# I CAN READ ABOUT
# JOHNNY APPLESEED

Written by J.I. Anderson

Illustrated by
William Krasnoborski

**Troll Associates**

Take your pick. Red . . . green . . . yellow apples. Big apples . . . little apples . . . delicious apples. Take your pick . . . Apples grow just about everywhere in America.

It wasn't always that way. A long time ago, there were very few apples in America. Then a man called Johnny Appleseed came along. And this is his story.

Johnny Appleseed was a real person. His real name was John Chapman. He was born in 1774, in a small town near Boston, Massachusetts.

His family owned a farm, and Johnny's
favorite spot was the apple orchard.
In the spring of the year, he'd
sit under the trees, listen to the
birds, and smell the wonderful smells
of the apple blossoms.

In the summer, he'd care for the trees so they would give plenty of delicious apples in the fall.

Even when he was a man, Johnny was happy working in the apple
orchards. And when his work was done, he would watch
the wagons passing by.

They were going west, out west to a new land.
People told Johnny that they were going
to settle in a great new wilderness.
They talked about rich soil that
was good for growing things.

The more stories Johnny heard, the more curious he became.
He had never been away from his father's farm.
Now he wanted to see these new lands for himself.

"There aren't any apple orchards out West," said Mr. Chapman, hoping his son would stay home. Johnny was surprised. How could people not have apples to eat.

"Dad, that's a *good* reason for going," said Johnny.
"People *need* apples. I'll go west and plant
apple trees."

So off he went. He packed as many apple seeds
as he could carry. He took some books, and
he took an old cooking pot, which he
wore on his head for a hat.

He saw what America was really like in those days.
He walked over hills and valleys, and passed small towns. He walked
and walked for weeks and weeks . . . from Massachusetts
all the way to Pittsburgh, Pennsylvania.

The land was rich, and good for growing things. So Johnny settled in Pittsburgh. He bought some land, built a cabin, and started growing apple trees.

When people passed by, Johnny gave them apple seeds or small young seedlings to take with them.

"Plant these seeds when you get out West," Johnny called.

"And peace be with you."

But, all too often, people returned
with the sad tale that either they
had lost the seeds or that
the seedlings had died.

Johnny was sad. "There *must* be a way to get apple trees growing out West," he thought.

Then he had an idea—a wonderful idea.

"I shall go myself. The only way there will be apple trees is if I plant the seeds myself." So, once again, Johnny packed his seeds, and headed west.

Along the way, he stopped and planted his seeds.

Sometimes, he would rest at a farmer's cabin. Then, Johnny would plant apple seeds in the farmer's field.

Sometimes, Johnny would stay with friendly Indians. He knew how to use herbs to cure the sick, and he was always welcome. If he had time, he would plant some apple seeds, too.

But most of the time, Johnny was alone.
He slept in the forest, and ate the foods of the
forest—the plants, fruits, and nuts. And every animal
in the forest was his friend. He was kind and careful
with all the creatures he met.

The years passed quickly.
Johnny was no longer a young man.
His hair grew thick and tangled.
His clothes grew torn and ragged.
And the pot on his head turned
rusty and dented.

You can imagine how strange Johnny looked
when he walked into a new town, and knocked on someone's door.
But Johnny was always welcome. There was
something about him that people liked.

People began to tell stories about Johnny. Folks loved to talk about the "apple man," and the orchards he planted. Whenever people talked about Johnny, they called him "Johnny Appleseed."
He was becoming a legend.

They especially liked to tell stories about
Johnny and his animal friends. And the story they
liked best was the story about Johnny and his friend the
wolf. It seems that one day Johnny was planting
apple seeds in a clearing in a forest.

Suddenly, he heard
a growling noise
behind him. Johnny turned
and saw a gray wolf
caught in a
hunter's trap.

"Don't be afraid. I won't hurt you," Johnny said gently.
Then he forced the trap open.

The wolf's leg was bleeding badly from
the trap. Johnny quickly put a bandage
on the wolf's leg. The wolf was so
grateful that he licked Johnny's hand.

Johnny nursed the wolf back to health. When the wolf's leg
was better, Johnny packed his things and started to leave.
As Johnny started to walk away, the wolf got up and followed
him. He wanted to be Johnny's friend.

From that day on, Johnny and the wolf traveled together.
The wolf helped Johnny plant his seeds, and
Johnny taught the wolf to be
kind and gentle.

Farmers welcomed Johnny into
their homes. They liked
to hear the story of how
Johnny found the wolf. They
liked to hear about the towns
Johnny had visited and the
things he had seen.

The farmers' children loved the little presents
Johnny always gave them—the bright ribbons for the
girls and smooth stones for the boys. And they
liked to play with Johnny's gray wolf.

One sad day
a terrible thing happened.
Johnny and the wolf had traveled to a
strange part of the country. They walked up to
a cabin in the woods. A man with a gun was at the door.

Johnny called out.
But it was too late.
A shot rang out and
the wolf fell dead
at Johnny's feet.

The man had never heard of Johnny Appleseed. He did not know that the wolf was Johnny's friend. Sadly, Johnny carried the wolf away and buried him in a quiet place in the forest.

"Goodbye, my friend," he said.

Then Johnny turned and walked on alone.

There was still work to do. Johnny traveled through Ohio, Kentucky, Indiana, and walked as far west as Missouri planting his apple seeds. But he was growing old and tired. He was over 70 years old, and he had been planting apple trees for many, many years.

It was time to rest.
One spring day, Johnny stopped at an orchard in
Indiana. He had planted that orchard many years
before. The sweet apple blossoms reminded
him of his boyhood. He decided to
sit under the tree, and smell
the wonderful smells of
the apple blossoms.

Folks wondered what had happened to Johnny Appleseed. He was not seen around the countryside again. Some say that he died. But, everywhere they looked, people saw Johnny's mark upon the land.

Wonderful apple trees were growing everywhere . . . and everyone knew they were the work of one man . . . a man called Johnny Appleseed.